The Little Rippers

Volume 2:
Go West, Little Rippers!

By: Rebecca Munsterer

Novel Nibble Publishing
Norwich, Vermont

Novel Nibble Publishing, August 2015
Copyright @ 2015 by Rebecca Munsterer Sabky

Published in the United States by Novel Nibble, Vermont
August 2015

Illustrations by Ryan Hueston and Molly Gentine

Printed by CreateSpace, An Amazon.com Company

"For in Colorado,
The snow drifts are deeper.
The bison are woolly,
The ski slopes are steeper.

The crests of the mountain,
Pierce western skies.
A landscape of colors,
Paint every sunrise.

Yet, many are called,
By whispering wind.
To climb the tall peaks,
Then start to descend.

Mountains are tall,
But friendship is bigger.
Your time is now,
Go West, *Little Rippers*."

-Grandpa

*For Mary Margaret Gentine,
the sweetest Little Ripper.*

Table of Contents

Chapter 1:
Pack It Up

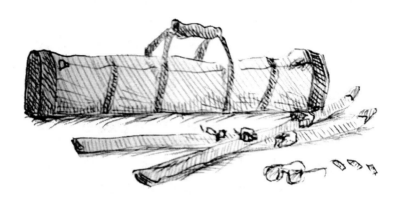

Max Beckett couldn't remember if he packed his long underwear. He remembered packing his gloves. He remembered packing his ski boots. And, of course, he was already wearing his favorite green jacket. But for some reason, he wasn't sure about his underwear.

"Molly, do you remember if I packed my long johns?" he asked his older sister.

"Ew," said Molly as she crinkled her nose. "I don't pay attention to your underwear."

Max's grandfather smiled as he looked at Max's overstuffed suitcase. "I'm sure they are in your bag somewhere. It looks like you packed an elephant in there."

Max knew he had overpacked for his trip. But he had never been to Colorado, so he had no idea what to expect. In addition to all of his ski clothes, he also brought a bathing suit, a pair of sunglasses, and his collection of baseball cards, just in case.

"It's too late to turn around now anyway," Molly said as she stood up from her seat in the airport. "They're calling our seat numbers. It's time to board!"

Max and Molly had never before been on an airplane, never mind a flight all the way from Pennsylvania to Colorado. They were excited about their trip, but they were even more excited about reuniting with their friend, Jenna Duke.

They had met Jenna during a ski trip in Vermont with a group called the Little Rippers. Jenna and her mom had generously invited the Little Rippers for a weekend of big mountain skiing at their home.

Molly had used all of her dog-walking money to save up for her airline ticket. And Max had sold his bicycle, *Blue Betty*, to help pay for his ticket. Grandpa had agreed to chaperone the kids, as he lived in Colorado when he was much younger and loved the western mountains.

"I call the window seat," Max announced as he boarded the plane.

"I want the aisle seat," Molly said.

"Well, I guess I'll sit in the middle," Grandpa shrugged.

Once they were seated in row nineteen, Max and Molly explored their surroundings. Max turned on his overhead light to read the gadget catalogue he found in the seat pocket. Molly discovered a tray table that flipped down from the seat in front of her.

"Trays up for take-off," a flight attendant instructed Molly as she walked down the aisle. "You can put your tray back down when I serve drinks and snacks later in the flight," she smiled.

"Oh, boy, takeoff!" Molly smiled.

"Oh double boy, drinks and snacks!" Max giggled.

"Now kids, be sure to look out the window as we fly. The topography of Pennsylvania is going to look very different from Colorado," Grandpa instructed.

"What's topography?" Max asked.

"It's the mountains and the rivers and the way the earth looks," Molly said in a matter-of-fact tone.

"Very good, Molly," replied Grandpa. "You must have been paying attention in school."

"I have," said Molly. "I also know that Colorado is the Centennial State. It became a state one hundred years after the Declaration of Independence was signed. And in order to get there from Pennsylvania, we're going to fly over the Mississippi River. M-I-S-S-I-S-S-I-P-P-I."

Max rolled his eyes at his know-it-all sister. "Grandpa, tell me more about when you lived in Colorado."

Grandpa smiled. "It was a long time ago. I was working as a geologist."

Molly leaned toward Max. "A geologist is someone who studies rocks."

"I know, I know," Max dismissed his sister. "Go on, Grandpa. Tell me more!"

"Well, I helped a group of engineers figure out where to build tunnels in the mountains. They needed someone who knew about rock formations. I did a lot of work, but I also did a lot of skiing," he winked at his grandson. "Now, look out your window. We're about to lift off the runway."

The plane flew toward the sky as Max and Molly watched from their seats. The houses in Pennsylvania slowly became miniature until they were hard to see. After one hour of looking out the window, Max started to doze off into sleep. Molly had already fallen asleep, and was leaning on Grandpa's shoulder.

Two hours later, Grandpa shook both Molly and Max awake. "Kids, it's time to land."

"Landing?" Max sat up quickly from his seat. "But I didn't see the Mississippi River, and I didn't get a drink or a snack."

"Me neither," Molly yawned as she wiped her eyes.

"The flight attendant gave me two extra bags of pretzels," Grandpa replied as he handed the snacks to the kids. "There's the airport. Hold on, we're about to touch down!"

To Max's surprise, the Denver airport looked like a snow-capped mountain range. It had peaks which resembled ski mountains. Max knew that he was in for a big adventure if even the airport looked like a ski area.

"This is going to be the best trip of my life," he whispered to himself.

Chapter 2:
Bison and Bighorn

Max and Molly had traveled to five states in their lifetime. But all five states were east of their home state of Pennsylvania. While they had read books and seen pictures of Colorado, they were still tremendously excited to actually be there.

After collecting their oversized ski bags in a special nook of Denver airport, Max, Molly and Grandpa picked up their rental car. The rental car had special snow tires for mountain roads.

However, as they started driving through Denver, Max realized that they had a problem. "Grandpa? Are you sure we're in the right place? The land looks awfully flat, and there's no snow anywhere."

"Look that way, silly," Molly said to her little brother as she pointed out the front window.

Max looked forward. A border of tall, jagged mountains caught the reflection of the setting sun. The mountain tops were snow-covered, but the snow appeared golden-pink in the light of the sun. Max was immediately both impressed and intimidated. "We're going up there?" he asked.

"Yessiree," replied Grandpa. "But we have a long ride ahead of us. We have to drive through the plains first. Keep your eye out for bison."

"I've never seen a bison," Max responded.

"Well you have now," Molly laughed. "Look!" She pointed out the window to a herd of bison. They were roaming on a nearby range.

"Holy moly!" Max screamed. "They look like woolly bullies!"

"There's a lot more to see as we head up the canyon. Keep your eyes open," Grandpa encouraged.

Grandpa's rental car made its way through the Colorado plains and up the foothills of the mountains. As they traveled through the foothills, the terrain outside the window became more and more ragged. As the land became steeper, the car curved and swerved to meet the road.

Around the third curve of the road, Max saw a ski area with at least four chairlifts. "Wow, Grandpa! Look at the size of that mountain! Is that Big Grizzly?"

"Nope," Grandpa replied. "That's Little Bear. We've got four more ski areas to pass before we reach Big Grizzly. It's the biggest and the baddest of all of the mountains!"

"Baddest?" Max asked.

"The steepest and the deepest," Molly said with a smile. "Jenna told me that it has the highest elevation in the entire state!"

"The entire state?" Max worried to himself. He knew that he could ski big mountains like Powderhound in Vermont, but he wasn't sure he could handle the steeps of the West. Little Bear Mountain even looked big to him.

The car continued to climb the mountain highway. They saw rock quarries in the side of the mountain, and runaway truck ramps. They saw a few bighorn sheep and even a mountain goat, poised on top of a teeny tiny rock.

"He's barely standing on the rock ridge," Max worried. "He's going to fall."

"Not with his toes," Grandpa explained. "He's the best climber in the area."

"So cool!" said Max.

"Now, get ready for my favorite part of the drive," Grandpa announced. "I helped work on this tunnel years ago. Get ready to go underground!"

Max had always loved tunnels. He was excited by the idea of a passageway through the mountainside. But he had never been in a tunnel as long as the tunnel in the Colorado canyon. At one point, it was so dark, he couldn't even see his sister sitting next to him.

"I see the light at the end of the tunnel," Molly exclaimed as the car neared the exit.

As they drove, Max noticed how much more snow was on the ground. Near the airport, there was no snow. Near the foothills, there were only a couple of inches. But, now, near the top of the mountain, there were at least a few feet of fluffy white snow. After driving to the very top of the mountain range at sunset, Grandpa's car finally slowed. "There it is," he announced as he pulled into a parking lot. "Big Grizzly!"

Max's eyes opened wide as he looked at the ski area. The mountain was so large, he could barely see the top and the bottom without moving his head. There were at least ten trails coming down the front of the mountain and at least five lifts near the base. At the base of the ski trails was a three-story log lodge, covered with snow hanging from its slanted roof. A red-painted sign hung from the lodge. It read, *"Welcome To Big Grizzly Mountain, Where The Skiing Is GRRRReat!"*

"GRRRReat!" Max laughed.

"Oh, Grandpa," Molly said in disbelief, "it's beautiful!"

"It sure is, kids. It looks the same as it did forty years ago, with a couple of new lifts perhaps," Grandpa responded. "Now, let's get to Jenna's house. The directions say to drive up this access road."

Grandpa drove up an old dirt road which ran parallel to the beginner's chairlift. The road was snow-dusted, with no other cars in sight. After about a half mile, the car pulled up to a house which appeared to be located on the slope itself.

Chapter 3:
Slope Side

As soon as Grandpa, Molly, and Max exited the car, the front door to the house popped open and Jenna stood in the doorway. She grinned from ear to ear. "You made it!" Jenna sprinted to her friends to give them a hug.

"Jenna," Molly said as she squeezed her old friend. "It's so good to see you!"

Max took his turn to hug Jenna. "And it's so good to finally see Colorado! It's unbelievable!"

Wyatt ran out of the front door behind Jenna. "Max and Molly are here!"

"It's a Little Rippers reunion!" said Chase who quickly followed.

Max and Molly were thrilled to see the other two Little Rippers, Wyatt and Chase. Wyatt was an expert water skier from Florida. Chase lived in Vermont, and was one of the fastest snow skiers that Max and Molly knew. Both Wyatt and Chase had arrived to Jenna's house earlier that day and Jenna and her family had picked them up at the airport.

"Welcome, everyone," Jenna's mom appeared at the front door. She looked similar to Jenna with lots of freckles and a welcoming smile. She gave everyone, including Grandpa, a hug. "Come on in, and make yourself comfortable. We're so glad you are here!"

The inside of Jenna's home was warm and comforting. A large fireplace crackled from the far end of the living room. A long marble counter, covered with bowls of fruit and cookie jars, stood in the kitchen. And a large rack of moose antlers hung on the living room wall.

"Are those real?" Max asked as he looked at the antlers.

"They are," said a voice from down the stairs. A girl slightly taller than Jenna with much longer brown hair appeared. "My mom found them on a ski trail. The moose chased all of the skiers down the mountain, and then left his antlers behind as a reminder to stay off his trail."

"Really?" Max asked in terror.

"Jackie," said Jenna's mom, "don't make up fibs." She turned toward Max. "There are moose out here, but they never bother the skiers. I bought the antlers at an antique shop in Boulder."

"Oh," Max said, embarrassed to have been frightened.

"Max, Molly, this is my big sister, Jackie," Jenna said proudly. Then she whispered, "Jackie is in sixth grade."

"I'm in middle school," Jackie boasted. "And I already know everything about you. Wyatt and Chase told me everything on our drive back from the airport. For example, I know that you are much younger than me."

"Well, do you know that I can say the alphabet backwards, I can cartwheel on one hand, and I can play the guitar?" Molly smiled coyly as she put her hand out to shake hands.

"You can play the guitar?" Jackie asked, impressed. "I play the guitar!" She lightly slapped Molly's hand with a special handshake. *"Boom, Bam, Clapping Hands.* This is what I do with all the kids I like."

Max spoke up. "Well, I can play the trumpet, I can juggle three oranges at one time, and I can touch my tongue to my nose." Max lifted his tongue to touch the tip of his nose. "See?" he said as he put out his hand.

"Ew," said Jackie as she just gave it a normal shake. Then, she turned back to Molly. "You should ski with me and my friends tomorrow. We're called the Pink Ponytails and we're all middle school friends. The other girls are so cool. We're going to start a rock band someday."

"Wow, a rock band!" Molly exclaimed. As she responded, she noticed Jenna's frown. "But maybe I should just ski with the Little Rippers."

Molly didn't have much time to consider Jackie's offer since Chase grabbed her arm. "Come see the best part of the house!" he said as he started running toward the stairs.

"Wait up!" Wyatt said as he followed Chase. He slid down the rail of the stairs, and landed on his feet on the bottom floor.

"Wait for me!" Max said as he tried to slide down the rail. But, after only a few feet, he toppled sideways.

"Are you okay, Max?" Jenna's mom asked as she helped him to his feet.

"I'm fine. I'm good at falling. Wait until you see me on the slopes!" he laughed.

Once Grandpa, Max and Molly arrived downstairs, Chase flipped on the outside lights and they all peered through the window. One of the Big Grizzly ski trails was directly in Jenna's backyard.

"Slope side skiing!" Grandpa exclaimed. "Mrs. Duke, we are so lucky to be your guests."

"I'm so lucky to have you! Now, it's time to get some sleep. The forecast calls for blue skies and white trails tomorrow! Grandpa, you'll sleep in the guest room on the second floor. And the kids will sleep in the bunk beds in the den!"

"I call a top bunk!" Chase announced.

"I call a bottom bunk!" said Wyatt.

"I call any bunk," Max smiled. "I'd sleep on the bathroom floor just to wake up slope side!"

Molly nodded her head in agreement. "Tomorrow is going to be the best day of skiing ever!"

Chapter 4:
Ponytails

The next morning, Chase was the first person out of bed. He jumped down from his top bunk and yelled loudly at his friends. "Wake up, Rippers, it's time to ski."

The sound of Chase's voice carried all the way through the house. Grandpa was already in the kitchen cooking breakfast. "Good morning, Little Rippers! Rise and shine!" he yelled downstairs.

The Little Rippers and Jackie found their way to the kitchen. Jenna's mom joined the group just as breakfast was being served. "Are these the famous Lumberjack Pancakes that I've heard so much about?"

"Not today," Grandpa smiled. "When I lived out here, we made Colorado Crepes. They're filled with energy to keep you warm and active."

"De-lish," said Chase as he took a bite.

Mrs. Duke sat at the counter with the kids. "Now before I hand out your lift tickets, I want to go over some safety reminders."

"Oh, Mom. Not the safety talk again," Jackie complained.

"You know that being on Ski Patrol means that I take safety seriously," Mrs. Duke replied.

"You are on Ski Patrol?" Wyatt asked. "That's awesome! You get to save people's lives."

"Well, I prefer that they don't get themselves in trouble in the first place," Mrs. Duke smiled. "That's why I want you to stay out of Bear Basin until the afternoon. You should warm-up properly before heading into the powder bowl."

"Bear Basin?" Max asked as his eyes grew wide.

"It's only the best powder bowl in all of Colorado," Jackie said.

"Powder? That's so cool!" Molly said with a smile.

"It is cool," said Mrs. Duke, "but it can also be dangerous. That's why I don't want you skiing back there without an adult. Grandpa can take you all there this afternoon. But this morning, stick to the main mountain. Jenna and Jackie will be your guides."

"Yeah, we know all of the mountain trails!" Jenna said enthusiastically. "They are all named after animals! Goldfish. Caribou. Lion. Hammerhead. Bunny."

"I want to ski Hammerhead!" Chase yelled. "It sounds fierce, just like me!"

"I think I'll stick to Bunny," Grandpa laughed. "But just in case, I brought some trail maps. You should all take one in case we get separated."

All of the Little Rippers took a trail map from Grandpa. Max was given the last trail map from Grandpa's pocket. "Make sure you don't lose this map, young man," Grandpa said with a stern voice.

"Okay," Max said. "I'll need this map since I'm going to ski every trail at the mountain."

Jackie was unamused. "The Pink Ponytails are going to be here soon. Can we go, Mom?"

"Of course! Of course!" Mrs. Duke said as she handed out lift tickets to the kids. "Have fun out there kids! I'll be with the Ski Patrol, but I'll be looking for you on the slopes!"

The Little Rippers fastened their tickets to their jackets and then brought their empty plates to the dishwasher. Moments later, they collected their ski gear and stepped outside to the slope.

As Molly clicked into her bindings, Jackie approached her. "I love your ponytail." She reached into her pocket and pulled out a pink ribbon. She handed it to Molly. "This might look nice in your hair. I'm wearing one too, see!" She turned her helmet to show off her ribbon.

"Wow, thanks!" said Molly. She carefully tied the ribbon into her ponytail.

"Do you have one for me?" Jenna asked.

"Nope," Jackie said. "That was my last one."

Suddenly, three girls in matching white helmets skied over to Jackie. They all had ponytails with pink ribbons peeking out of the back of their helmets.

Jackie smiled at her friends. "Morning, Pink Ponytails!"

One of the Pink Ponytails looked at Wyatt. "Who are these kids?"

"They're the Little Rippers," Jackie said. "Isn't that cute? The *Little* Rippers."

"But we're big mountain skiers," Chase piped up.

"You're just a little boy, Chase," Jackie said. "You wouldn't be able to ski with us."

"Wanna bet?" Chase asked. "Catch me if you can!" Chase pushed off the snow and sped toward the chairlift.

"I'm on your tail already," Wyatt said as he chased his friend.

"Want to come ski with us, Molly?" Jackie asked.

"I think I'll stay with my brother and Jenna," Molly replied.

"No, you definitely want to come with us," Jackie replied. "The Pink Ponytails should ski together."

"See you later, I guess," Molly said to Jenna as she skied away with Jackie.

Jenna was pretty upset. Jackie had a tendency to exclude her, but now she was taking away her friend as well.

Grandpa could sense her sore feelings. "You know, Max and I really need a tour guide. Will you ski with us, Jenna?"

"Okay," said Jenna. "The Pink Ponytails will probably want me to ski with them tomorrow. But for now, I'll show you all around my mountain."

Chapter 5:
Pick a Trail

Big Grizzly was the largest mountain Max had ever seen. As he sat on the lift between Grandpa and Jenna, he clutched the safety bar.

"If we fall off, we'll fall into that stream," Max announced.

"That's nothing," Jenna said. "We're not even to mid-mountain yet. When we get to the top, it's really just the bottom of the other lift."

"The top is really the bottom? This is so confusing," Max replied. "I wish Molly was here, Grandpa."

"I wish my sister was here too," Jenna agreed. "Jackie is the coolest, but she doesn't really like having me around."

Grandpa smiled wisely at Max and Jenna. "I'm sure both of your sisters wish they were skiing with you right now."

As soon as the words came out of Grandpa's mouth, the Pink Ponytails, Chase, Wyatt, and Molly sped by underneath the chair. They were giggling and howling as they chased each other down the slope.

"Hey Molly!" Max yelled below.

"Looking good, Jackie," Jenna screamed down from the chairlift.

But the girls didn't hear them. They just skied right by.

Grandpa sensed their disappointment. "Come on, kids, it's time to get off the lift."

After taking the second lift to the tippy top of Big Grizzly, Max couldn't believe the view. "I think I can see Pennsylvania from here."

"Which run do you want to take?" Jenna asked. "We have a few options. Tortoise? Hedgehog? Snake?"

"Let's take Snake. It sounds long and winding!" Max replied.

Snake trail was nearly a mile long. Max and Grandpa followed Jenna as the trail turned from right to left, then from left to right. Max had forgotten how well his Grandpa could ski, but was quickly reminded as he tried to imitate his wide, perfect turns. When they reached the bottom, Max took a long gasp of air.

"That. Was. Awesome," he huffed.

"And that was a green circle," Jenna said. "That's the easiest trail we have at Big Grizzly. The next run we're going to take is Wolverine!"

After two more runs, Max was finally getting the knack of Colorado skiing. He remembered to breathe. He remembered to keep his hands forward. And he remembered to have fun with his old pal, Jenna.

Grandpa was also remembering to have fun. But after having knee surgery earlier that year, he also knew not to push himself too hard. "Kids, I'm going to ski down and rest my knee for a few runs. I'll meet you at Jenna's house for lunch. Max, make sure to use your trail map if you need it."

Max patted his pocket to make sure he could still feel his map. "Will do," he yelled as his Grandpa skied down the slope.

"Let's go to the Tram!" Jenna announced. "That's probably where the Pink Ponytails are skiing."

"What's the Tram?" Max asked as Jenna skied away. He followed her without an answer to his question.

"You'll see," she yelled over her shoulder.

Max thought the Tram looked like a flying microwave. It was a large enclosed lift on a cable that carried dozens of skiers at one time. When Max followed Jenna to the lift line, he was thrilled to see some very familiar faces. The Pink Ponytails and the rest of the Little Rippers were over by the Tram.

"Max!" Molly yelled from the lift line. "Over here!"

Max was surprised to see Molly and the others holding their skis in their hands. To load the Tram, skiers had to hand-carry their own skis and poles. Max and Jenna quickly clicked out of their skis and walked over to their friends and sisters. "Isn't Big Grizzly awesome?" Max asked the group.

"We just skied two non-stop mogul runs!" Wyatt exclaimed.

"It was just our warm-up," Jackie said, matter-of-fact, as she re-tied her ponytail. "Now, we're going to ski the hard runs."

"Terrific," Jenna exclaimed. "We'll join you."

The Little Rippers and the Pink Ponytails boarded the Tram in single file. They carried both their skis and poles onboard. Molly and Max stood near the window of the Tram, and marveled at the view below. The Tram glided on a cable far above streams, trees, and big boulders. When it reached the top, it slowed down for passengers to exit.

"Out of our way," Jackie said as she elbowed her sister toward the exit. "We want to beat you to the fresh powder in Bear Basin."

"But Jackie," Jenna yelled, "we're not allowed in Bear Basin without an adult."

"Don't be such a baby," Jackie yelled back. "Molly, Chase, Wyatt, are you coming with us?"

Max approached his sister who was putting on her skis. "Molly, Jenna's mom specifically told us to stick to the main mountain this morning."

"I know, I know. But I'm afraid to say no to Jackie," Molly responded.

"Well, I'm not afraid," Max said. He carried his skis and poles over to Jenna's big, bossy, sister. "Jackie, we're not allowed to ski in Bear Basin alone. It's too dangerous."

"Fine," said Jackie. "None of you have to come with us. See you later, *Little* Rippers." Jackie and the Pink Ponytails skied away toward a back trail. Their pink ponytails bobbed behind their helmets as they disappeared over the edge of the mountain.

"Rats," Molly said. "There go my friends."

"They are not your friends," Chase said. "They are just a group of silly girls."

"I'm your friend, Molly," Jenna said. "And I want to ski with you."

"I know, I know, but those girls are in middle school. They're so cool."

"We'll catch up to them later," Wyatt said. "Now, we need to find our way down from here."

"I know," said Jenna. "We can take Moose to Gopher to Giraffe. Or is it Giraffe to Moose to Gopher? Oh, gosh, I can't remember."

"Don't worry," Max insisted. "We can just look at a trail map." Max pulled his trail map out of his pocket and studied the piece of paper. "I don't see Giraffe on my map. In fact, I don't see Moose or Gopher either."

"Let me see," Jenna said. Jenna peeked at Max's map. His map didn't look familiar. "Wait a second," she said as she pulled her map out of her pocket. "Look! Your map is different."

The Little Rippers all peered at Max's map. It certainly showed trails on the mountain, but there was a long red line which squiggled back and forth on the paper and then ended with a big, red, X.

"That's funny," Chase leaned in and pointed to the X. "This looks like a treasure map. I bet that X stands for something, just like a pirate treasure hunt."

Molly shook her head. "I don't know. It could just be a misprint."

"There's only one way to find out," Wyatt smiled slyly.

Max inspected his map. He pointed his gloved finger down the red line from the top of Tram. "It looks like there is a secret trail nearby."

"I know the front of this mountain like the back of my hand," Jenna said. "And I've never heard of a secret trail."

Max took a deep breath. Grandpa had told him to pay close attention to his ski map. For whatever reason, he believed that they should follow the line.

"Little Rippers, we're not going to Bear Basin. But we are all about to have a real Colorado adventure." Max pushed his poles toward a nearby trailhead named Bison. One by one, the Little Rippers followed.

Chapter 6:
Big Mountain Skiing

Max stopped near the trailhead for Bison and inspected his magic map. "According to the red line, the secret trail begins behind that big boulder."

Molly and the Little Rippers inspected the nearby boulder. It was at least fifteen feet tall and equally wide. There were no tracks anywhere in sight.

"Well, there's only one way to find out what's on the other side." Chase skied around the boulder and disappeared.

The Little Rippers followed Chase around the boulder. To their surprise, on the other side of the rock, there was a secret trail.

"This is awesome," Jenna whispered. "I've never seen this trail before!"

"Ya-hoo!" yelled Wyatt as he started skiing. "This is big mountain skiing, and we have the slope all to ourselves."

The Little Rippers skied behind Wyatt. The snow on the trail was untracked, perfect powder.

"Hold up!" Max yelled to the group as they approached a large evergreen tree. "That's the giant tree. It's on my map!"

Max pulled his map from his pocket and inspected the red line. "We need to go to the right of this tree, but then to the left of the next tree. Then to the right. Then to the left." Max looked up from his map. "We need to turn around ten giant evergreen trees."

"I can do that!" said Chase as he pushed off the snow and went to the right of the humongous evergreen. The tree was so large it made Chase look miniature.

"Does he ever wait?" Molly asked as she rolled her eyes and followed her friend.

The Little Rippers skied to the right of the first big evergreen, then to the left of the next. They weaved and bobbed amongst the oversized trees. Max pretended like he was skiing around large animals like moose and bison.

After ten big turns, the kids stopped and took a breath. The slope below became incredibly steep. It was the steepest slope Molly had ever seen. "I don't know if I can ski any further. I think I would have a better chance of getting down by foot."

"But we are almost to the X," Max exclaimed, excited. "Now we just need to go…" he pointed his finger all the way over to the other side of the slope, "…over there!"

"Oh, phooey!" Chase said. "How are we going to get over there?"

"That's a traverse!" Jenna exclaimed. "We traverse in Colorado when we cross a steep slope. You just point your skis sideways across the mountain, and push your way to the other side."

Chase leaned over the side of the steep slope and whispered to Max. "Just don't fall, since you might not be able to get back up."

The Little Rippers traversed carefully, following each other one by one. Jenna led the group, setting a track with her skis. Traversing was quite frightening at first, but once the Little Rippers realized that they could follow Jenna's tracks, it became easier. When they reached the other side of the mountain, they carefully balanced on the steep slope like mountain goats.

"Can we ski down now?" Molly announced. "I'm getting dizzy."

"Nope. We have to find the X," Chase said enthusiastically.

Max pulled his map out of his pocket one more time. He could tell that they were standing exactly where they needed to be. He looked around him. A couple feet away, he noticed a mysterious opening in the trail.

"I think I found it," Max announced. "But I'm not sure what *it* really is."

Chapter 7:
X Marks the Spot

The Little Rippers had found the X on the map. It appeared to be the entrance to a tunnel in the snow. It had been concealed by snow drifts and fallen trees, and was very difficult to see if you weren't looking for it. But the Little Rippers were looking for it, and now Max had found it.

"Wow!" Max exclaimed to himself. "A secret tunnel!"

"It must have been a shortcut for the folks who built Big Grizzly. I've heard that they created tunnels to easily bring supplies from one side of the mountain to the other," Jenna announced. "It looks like it has been abandoned for a while though."

"I don't know if we should go in there," Molly said as she peered inside.

"But that's where the map is telling us to go! And Jenna's mom said we could ski anywhere except Bear Basin this morning." Chase said. "We've got to try it!"

"I don't know," said Molly. "There could be bears hibernating down there. Maybe that's why this mountain is called Big Grizzly!"

"HELLO IN THERE, BEARS!" Chase yelled into the tunnel. His voice echoed down the chamber. Chase waited a moment and then smiled at Molly. "See? No response! No bears! I'm going for it!" Chase pushed off with his poles and dropped into the tunnel. "Yahoo!" he yelled from below.

"How is it down there?" Max yelled into the tunnel as his voice echoed.

"DAARRKK!" screamed Chase.

"I have a flashlight on my keychain!" Jenna said as she reached into her pocket. "I keep it for nights when I sneak to the kitchen for peanut butter cookies."

"Yum, peanut butter cookies," Wyatt said.

"Hey, focus on the flashlight!" Chase yelled back up from the tunnel. "There's only a dim light coming from the other side of the tunnel, and I don't like not being able to see."

Jenna flipped the keychain flashlight to the ON switch, and attached the whole keychain to her jacket zipper. Then, she dropped into the tunnel. "Whoa!" her voice echoed up to the other Rippers.

"What is it?" Molly yelled. "Did you wake a bear?"

Jenna's giggles came from underground. "No, silly. It's just an awesome ski tunnel down here! Come on! We'll all ski together!"

Max and Wyatt slowly skied into the tunnel. Molly was the last to join the group. As she slid in, she inspected her surroundings. Jenna's flashlight was strong enough to illuminate the entire area. The tunnel looked silver and shiny with a fresh coat of untracked snow on the bottom of its barrel. "I don't like being underground, but this is pretty cool," Molly agreed.

"It's also pretty windy," Wyatt said. "Listen to the howl of the tunnel." The wind barreling up the tunnel made a low, whistling noise like a hum.

Molly smiled to herself. "That's why there is snow in the tunnel! The wind is blowing snow in here!"

"It's the perfect ski tunnel!" Chase exclaimed as he tried to ski. But as hard as he pushed, he only went at a snail's pace. "I'm pretty slow," he said as he pushed against the wind.

Wyatt agreed. "Me too. This is one windy tunnel."

"Not for me," Molly leaned forward on her skis and tucked her arms in next to her. Her skis took off quickly down the tunnel. "Whoa! Whoa! WHOA! I'm going superfast! Wahoo!"

Chase and Wyatt dropped down into tucks as well. All of a sudden, their skis increased speed. "Yippee!" screamed the boys.

"It's a tucking tunnel!" Jenna yelled over to Max. "Just like the wind simulators that the Olympic ski racers use to train! All we need to do is tuck!" Jenna jumped into position and started barreling down the tunnel. "Away we go!"

Max readjusted his goggles and tightened his ski boots. He wanted to be ready for the speed. "Three-two-one and away I go!" he yelled to himself.

The Tucking Tunnel was fun… *really* fun… and much more of an adventure than any of the Little Rippers had anticipated. It was a topsy-turvy ride, which was more exciting than any roller coaster or waterslide. It snaked around underground, weaseling down the slope from one side to the other.

The Little Rippers skied closely next to Jenna so that her flashlight illuminated their way downhill. They rode the curves while staying in their tucks.

Max felt like he was in an Olympic Downhill course as he held his tuck. The tunnel flew by as he concentrated on each curve. Sometimes he leaned right. Sometimes he leaned left. But all the time, he leaned forward. The more forward he leaned, the faster he went.

After a few minutes, the light grew brighter in the tunnel. Jenna and the rest of the Rippers knew they were approaching the exit. "Hold on, Little Rippers," she yelled to the back of the pack. "I think our ride is nearly over!"

Jenna held on tight as the tunnel spit her into the air. She landed on the ski slope with a thump. The other Rippers landed in a similar fashion. "Well, that was quite a ride!" Jenna giggled as she gave her friends a high five.

"Let's do that again!" Molly cheered before turning around. "Hey, where did the Tucking Tunnel go?"

The Little Rippers turned to look at the Tucking Tunnel. As soon as they had exited the tunnel, a pile of snow had slid on the top of the tunnel to cover the exit. It was completely hidden on the trail.

"Wow," Max muttered to himself. "That's incredible. It completely disappeared."

Jackie, however, had reappeared. "Well, if it isn't the Little Rippers," she said. "You missed a great run in Bear Basin. It was deep and steep powder. The best I've ever skied. Too bad you missed it."

Jenna looked at her sister with disapproval. "Oh yeah, well we just skied…"

"…a run on the beginner's slope," Molly cut off Jenna. "It was boring. You would have thought it was too babyish."

Jenna understood what Molly was trying to do. She gave Molly a wink before turning back to her sister. "Yeah, it was real babyish."

"Well, we're going back up on the Tram," Jackie said as she started skiing toward the other Pink Ponytails. "Don't bother to follow us. You'll never keep up."

"We're going up the Tram, too," Jenna said. "And I bet we could beat you down the mountain."

"I'm sorry," Jackie said as she stopped in her ski tracks. "Did you just say that the Little Rippers could beat the Pink Ponytails down the mountain?"

"That's right!" Max replied. "The last ones down have to make hot chocolate at Jenna's house for the other group at lunchtime!"

"Good," Jackie replied. "Because we were just saying how thirsty we are for some hot cocoa. See you at the top."

Max looked back at the Little Rippers. Smiles filled their faces. They knew the Tucking Tunnel would give them a shortcut and an advantage.

The Tram ride to the top of Grizzly Mountain took a particularly long time. Partly because the Little Rippers couldn't wait to race down the mountain. Partly because they were smushed in the corner by the Pink Ponytails who were taking up lots of space.

"I'm sorry," Jackie said to Molly. "Are my poles in your way?"

"Not at all," Molly said rationally back. "I like being against the window. I have a better view."

"Hmph," said Jackie. "You know, you should really give me back my pink ribbon. It doesn't look good with your helmet."

"Here you go," Molly said as she untied the pink ribbon from her hair and handed it back to Jackie. Jackie put the ribbon in her pocket.

After the long ride up to the top of the mountain, the Little Rippers and the Pink Ponytails unloaded. They clicked on their skis, and lined up in two groups, facing each other. Jenna directly faced her sister.

"What are the rules?" Jenna asked.

"The rules are that there are no rules," Jackie said. "The first complete team to ski to the bottom of the mountain wins."

"Sounds good to me," said Jenna. She had never raced her sister before, and although she knew the Little Rippers secret trail, she was still incredibly nervous.

"It's a shame you won't go into Bear Basin," Jackie said. "It's clearly the fastest way to the bottom from here. You guys will be zig-zagging all over the green circle trails just to get to the bottom."

"Well, let's just hope our zig-zag is faster than your run," Chase added. "Now, on your mark, get set, GO!"

Chapter 8:
Shadows in the Dark

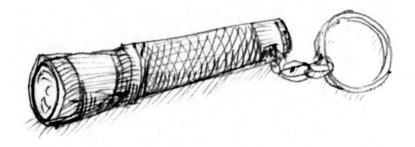

The Little Rippers had no time to spare as they skied to their secret trailhead. They dropped behind the big boulder, and skied as quickly as possible.

Max didn't even have to consult his map since he already committed the red line to memory. He led the Little Rippers through the giant evergreens. "Yahoo! Come on, Rippers! Ski fast!" he hollered as he bobbed and weaved around the green giants.

After successfully leaving tracks around every tree, the Little Rippers embarked on the steep traverse.

"Good work, team," Molly yelled as she led the pack horizontally across the slope in single file. "Now, keep moving! We need to traverse quickly."

Max's knees wobbled as he tried to remain steady. "Don't look down," he whispered to himself as he concentrated on balancing.

"Go faster," Chase yelled behind Max. "I'm catching up to you and I can't slow down!"

"I'm going as fast as I can!" Max screamed back.

"Well it's not fast enough," Chase announced as he inched closer to Max. There was no room to snowplow, so Chase couldn't help but gain momentum. Eventually, he skied right into Max.

Both Chase and Max landed in the snow with a thump.

Molly turned around in concern. "Are you two all right?"

Chase readjusted his skis parallel to the traverse tracks. He stood up, unharmed. Then he giggled. "I'm fine. The Colorado snow is soft for landing!"

Max shook snow off his green jacket and returned to his feet as well. "I'm okay too. But we better hurry up! We've got to beat the Pink Ponytails to the bottom."

Jenna was already on the move. She had skied right over to the tunnel entrance. "There's no time to spare. See you at the bottom everyone!"

"But we need your flashlight to see!" Wyatt yelled. "Wait for us!" Wyatt chased Jenna into the tunnel. Chase and Molly followed.

Max readjusted his goggles. But as he prepared to enter the tunnel, he realized that his pocket had opened during his fall, and his trail map was missing. "Hey guys, wait!" he yelled to the group.

But they couldn't hear him. They were already skiing through the tunnel, and the wind was too loud to hear his cries.

Max looked at the crater of snow where he and Chase fell. He didn't see the map, but he knew that he had to look for it. He leaned down on his skis and started brushing the powdery snow around on the ground. Finally, he saw the corner of the map. "Thank goodness," he muttered to himself. He pulled it out of the snow and zipped it safely in his pocket. Then, he hustled back over to the tunnel.

By the time Max entered the tunnel, the others were long gone. The tunnel was dark, with no sign of Jenna's flashlight. "Hello," Max yelled down the tunnel into the wind. "Jenna? Molly? Anybody?"

But there was no answer except for the hum of the wind. Max was scared. But he knew he had to be brave. He would have to ski the Tucking Tunnel in the dark. He didn't know any other way down the mountain, and he knew Jenna was counting on him to beat the Pink Ponytails.

Max leaned forward as his skis started sliding. There was just enough sunlight from the entrance of the tunnel to see the first curve. He leaned into the curve, and safely navigated his way. As he went further, the light drew dimmer. Everything looked gray and Max could barely see much more than the shadows of the tunnel walls.

Yet, he kept moving forward in his tuck, paying attention to the feeling of the snow below. When the tunnel curved left, he went left. When the tunnel curved right, he went right. When the tunnel went completely dark, he trusted his skis to guide him down the tracks which the other Little Rippers had already made.

Finally, he heard something echoing down the tunnel. It wasn't just the wind. "Max, Max! Are you in there?"

Max recognized Jenna's voice. He yelled back. "I'm in here!" Just hearing his friend made him want to get out of the tunnel faster. He leaned forward in his fiercest tuck and barreled down the tunnel. As the light became brighter, Max knew the exit was near.

"Whoa! Whoa! WHOA!" he cried as he was spit out of the tunnel and onto the snow.

"You made it!" Molly exclaimed as she skied over to her brother. "And you skied the entire tunnel in the dark!"

"That's totally radical!" Wyatt said as he high-fived his friend.

"I don't know if it was radical, but I do know that I'm happy to see the sun," Max laughed as he stood up. "Did we beat the Pink Ponytails?"

"No, you didn't beat us," Jackie announced as she stood at the bottom of the trail. "We've been down here for a full minute."

"Aw, shucks!" Max exclaimed in frustration. He was sure that the Tucking Tunnel would have helped them get to the bottom in record time.

"But you still won the race," Jackie said.

Jenna furrowed her brow in confusion. "What do you mean?"

"Mom saw us while she was patrolling in Bear Basin. We got in trouble, and she grounded us from skiing the rest of the weekend. She wouldn't even let us ski down here. The Ski Patrol snowmobiled us down the mountain."

"I knew it!" Jenna said. "I knew we would win."

Jackie looked at her sister with suspicion. "How did you get down here so fast? We would have still been skiing in Bear Basin for at least another ten minutes."

"Well, it was the…" Jenna turned around to point at the exit of the Tucking Tunnel. But once again, it was completely hidden by a sliding snow drift.

"It's a Little Rippers secret," Molly jumped in as she winked at Jenna.

Jackie looked down at the snow. "I understand," she replied. "I haven't been that nice to any of you. I probably wouldn't tell me your secret either."

Jenna looked at her sister closely. Jackie had tears in her eyes, and more importantly, she was missing something. "Jackie, where is your pink ribbon?"

Jackie hung her head. "The other girls are mad at me for getting them in trouble. They made me give back my pink ribbon."

Jenna reached into her pocket and pulled out three purple ribbons. "Well, I've been holding on to these for a while." She handed one to Molly. "I have one for my best Little Ripper friend."

Molly took the ribbon and tied it in her hair. "Thanks, Jenna."

Jenna tied the second ribbon in her own hair, and then outstretched the last ribbon to Jackie. "And I have one for my best sister." Jackie hesitated at first, but Jenna leaned over and tied the ribbon in her sister's hair. "Purple looks better on you anyway."

Jackie laughed. "Thanks, sis! You're all right."

At that moment, Jackie and the Little Rippers heard a familiar voice. It was Grandpa. It was almost noon, and he was hoping to take another run before lunch. "Hey kids, can I join you for a few turns?"

"Absolutely!" exclaimed Max. "First one to the Tram gets the top bunk!"

"No way!" said Chase as he started skiing to the chair as quickly as possible. Wyatt closely followed the other two boys.

"Are you coming, Jackie?" Jenna asked her sister.

"I have to sit this one out. Mom's rules," she smiled. "But I'd love to ski with you next weekend when I'm not grounded."

"Sounds good," said Jenna. "Now, go make us hot chocolate. We're going to be very thirsty at lunch," Jenna teased.

Jackie smiled back at her sister. As she walked away, Jenna admired the purple ribbon in her sister's hair.

Chapter 9:
Bear Basin And Back

Max considered telling Grandpa about the Tucking Tunnel. But he had made a pact with the other Little Rippers that they would keep their favorite run a secret.

"Which way do you want to go?" Grandpa asked as they unloaded the Tram.

Chase looked at the other Little Rippers. "Well, it's almost the afternoon and we've been waiting all day to ski someplace special," Chase smiled. "Bear Basin."

"Yeah, Bear Basin!" the other Rippers cheered.

"Okay, Rippers," Grandpa said. "But stay close to each other, keep an eye on the snow below, and most of all…"

"Have fun!" The Rippers yelled together.

The Little Rippers started skiing toward the access trail to the Bear Basin back bowl. However, Grandpa stopped for a moment to take in the view.

"What are you waiting for Grandpa?" Max yelled to his grandfather.

"Aw, I was just taking a walk down memory lane," Grandpa grinned at his grandson. "I used to work up here years ago. Now, let's go ski the powder!"

Skiing Bear Basin was even better than Max had dreamed. The powder was so fluffy that it felt like skiing through cotton.

Wyatt made big turns throughout the bowl, as if he were water skiing at home.

Chase went straight down the mountain pretending to be a downhill champion, gaining as much speed as possible.

Molly and Jenna made figure eight turns, taking their time to perfect their tracks.

And Max and Grandpa took their time to enjoy the view. Max wanted to remember exactly what Bear Basin looked like on such a bluebird day. He wanted to picture the large bowl of untracked powder, the occasional evergreen tree, and the swishing skis of his friends who bounced around the Basin like school kids in a playground.

Toward the end of the day, after a lunch of turkey sandwiches and homemade hot chocolate from Jackie, the Little Rippers were exhausted. They had skied dozens of runs in Bear Basin, and were getting ready for their final run. Max knew exactly what trail he wanted to take.

Grandpa's knees were ready for the hot tub, however. "Go ahead without me for the last run," Grandpa said.

"But Grandpa, we have a secret trail we think you'd really like to see," Max replied.

"Shh…" said Chase. "I thought that was a Little Rippers secret."

Grandpa smiled to himself. "I think you all should go on your secret run without me." He leaned in and whispered to Max. "I'm not a big fan of skiing in the dark anymore," he winked.

Max's eyes grew wide as the words came out of his grandfather's mouth. He knew exactly what Grandpa was trying to say.

"Let's go, Max!" Jenna hollered as she led the pack of Little Rippers to the Tram.

Max smiled to himself and chased his friends. "Coming!"

Two days later, Max, Molly and Grandpa packed their ski bags, and bid goodbye to Big Grizzly Mountain. They were exhausted from skiing nearly every trail on the mountain. They celebrated their long ski weekend with a final breakfast of Colorado Crepes with Jenna, Jackie, and Mrs. Duke, before thanking them for their hospitality.

Grandpa drove the long, winding road back down to the Denver plains, and after a flight back to Pennsylvania, Max found himself back home.

As Max unpacked his ski bag that evening, he remembered that he still had the secret trail map in his green jacket. He took the trail map from his pocket and hid it under his bed in his box of ski mementos. He placed it next to his speedy gold wax from Vermont and his old lift tickets.

Max knew one day he would be back to Big Grizzly. Until then, he wanted to keep that map in a very special place. Although he knew the trail to the Tucking Tunnel by heart, someday he would pass that magical map along to someone who loved adventure as much as the Little Rippers.

The End

Acknowledgments

I'd like to thank my friends and family who helped create the Little Rippers series.

Thank you to my friends who buy the book because they have kids who ski.

Thank you to my friends who buy the book, even though they don't have kids, nor do they ski.

Thank you to the ski areas who have welcomed me to book signings.

Thank you to Jamal, my husband-turned-Crepe recipe tester, a job he enjoys.

Thank you to my sister Molly, for learning how to draw bison and bunk beds.

Thank you to the fabulous Ryan Hueston for his talent and support.

Thank you to Ben, Gus, and Mary Margaret for being real Little Rippers.

Thank you to Jon for carrying Ben, Gus, and Mary Margaret down the slopes.

Thank you to my parents for paying for my lift tickets when I was a Little Ripper.

Thank you to the town of Norwich, Vermont for your support and inspiration.

Thank you to Mabel, the wonder dog, for keeping my feet warm while I wrote.

Thank you to the great state of Colorado for inspiring me as a youngster. You were my Disneyworld, but better.

Thank you to the New England Winter of 2015, whose negative temperatures forced me indoors to write, rather than playing in the snow.

And most of all, thank you to the readers. Writing a book is not easy. But sharing it is *really* fun. See you on the chairlift!

Appendix #1

Grandpa's Colorado Crepes

(Adapted recipe from Randi Buckley's kitchen)

Colorado Crepes are Grandpa's favorite treat to make for the Little Rippers! (Ask your parents for help when cooking in the kitchen.)

Ingredients
(Makes Eight Large Crepes)

1 cup sifted flour
2 cups milk
3 eggs, lightly beaten
Dash of vanilla extract
Butter for coating the skillet
Your choice of toppings: sliced bananas, powdered sugar, strawberries, mini chocolate chips, whipped cream, etc.

1. Beat the flour, milk, and eggs together. Mix until the batter has consistent texture.

2. Warm a skillet to medium-high heat. Melt butter on skillet to coat.

3. Slowly, add enough batter for one thin, flat crepe. When crepe has stiffened (approximately one minute), flip. Cook another minute on the other side.

4. Remove crepe from skillet, and add new batter for next crepe.

5. When finished, roll warm (but not hot) crepes, and cover with your choice of toppings. (Grandpa's favorite is strawberries and whipped cream.) Enjoy!

Little Rippers Activities

The Little Rippers traveled to Colorado for a wonderful adventure on the slopes of Big Grizzly. While traveling, they kept themselves occupied with these fun activities:

1. Molly's License Plate Game

While driving, Molly likes to look for state nicknames on license plates. Can you match the following states to their nicknames?

1. The Beehive State		a. New Jersey
2. The Garden State		b. Florida
3. The Sunshine State		c. Georgia
4. The Peach State		d. New Mexico
5. The Beaver State		e. Vermont
6. The Green Mountain State		f. Oregon
7. The Cactus State		g. Hawaii
8. The Aloha State		h. Utah

2. Max's Animal Alphabet Game

From bison to bighorn, Max enjoys learning about new animals. In fact, he keeps track of the creatures he sees, and hopes to one day have a list of animals whose names begin with every letter of the alphabet.

Can you name animals whose names begin with each letter of the alphabet? We'll help you get started:

A is for Aardvark
B is for Baboon
C is for Chipmunk
D is for Dolphin
E is for Elk…

3. Chase's Coloring Corner

Whether he's traveling by plane or by car, Chase passes the time by drawing. He's a doodler extraordinaire! Here are some doodles for you to try:

a. Doodle a mountain goat.
b. Doodle a ski mountain, complete with a base lodge.
c. Doodle an airplane
d. Doodle the Little Rippers! (Don't forget Max's green jacket and Molly's long ponytail!)

4. Jenna's Storytelling Surprise

When Jenna travels, she really enjoys storytelling with her mom and sister. They take turns sharing their own tales from the week. Tell your friends and family a story:

a. Tell them about something you tried for the first time this week.
b. Tell them about something you learned this week.
c. Tell them about something that you accomplished this week.
d. Tell them about a time you felt particularly challenged this week.
e. Tell them what you are looking forward to doing next week.

5. Wyatt's Physical Challenge

It's hard sitting in a car/bus/train/plane for a long period of time. Yet, Wyatt has some tricks for feeling good while traveling:

a. Leg Stretch: Lift your legs from the seated position until they are parallel with the floor. Point your toes straight and hold for ten seconds. Release and return your feet to the floor. Repeat ten times.

b. Head Roll: Drop your chin to your chest. Roll your head toward your right shoulder. Then drop your head as far backwards as possible. Then roll your head toward your left shoulder.

Complete a full circle head roll, careful to move your head slowly as you stretch.

c. Arm Stretch: Interlock fingers and outstretch hands vertically to the sky. Hold the pose for ten seconds. Release and drop your arms back to your side. Repeat four times.

Connect with us!

Are you a Little Ripper? We want to hear about your adventures on the slopes. Here are some ways to contact us:

1. Send us a letter! We love snail mail. Write to:
The Little Rippers Fan Club
P.O. Box 813
Norwich, Vermont
05055

2. Email us! Send us a picture, and you might be chosen as a featured Little Ripper on Facebook:
TheLittleRippers@Gmail.Com

3. Meet us in person! Author Rebecca Munsterer is signing books in ski lodges across the country. Ask your parents to check out our website and facebook page for a list of upcoming book tour dates! We would love to see you on the slopes!
www.thelittlerippers.com
www.facebook.com/LittleRippers

Thanks for being a Little Ripper!
Rip it up, and share the love of skiing!